James Topham Brady, Edward S. Hall

A Christmas Dream

James Topham Brady, Edward S. Hall

A Christmas Dream

ISBN/EAN: 9783337379049

Printed in Europe, USA, Canada, Australia, Japan

Cover: Foto ©Andreas Hilbeck / pixelio.de

More available books at **www.hansebooks.com**

\

CHRISTMAS DREAM.

BY

JAMES T. BRADY.

ILLUSTRATED BY EDWARD S HALL

NEW YORK:
PUBLISHED BY D. APPLETON & CO
443 AND 445 BROADWAY.
LONDON: 16 LITTLE BRITAIN
1861.

MR. STEPHEN C. MASSETT:

My Dear Stephen:

I dedicate to you this little volume. The sketch it contains was written some fourteen years ago, when you were a clerk in my office, and I did not suppose it would ever be presented in a more durable form. But as you retained a copy, took it with you on your various pilgrimages, and during the Christmas season read it to strangers even at the Antipodes, it seems to be yours more than mine, and I thus bestow it upon you. Mr. EDWARD S. HALL has made the book valuable by the admirable illustrations with which he has adorned it, and there may be some who will possibly derive gratification from having this frail memorial of him who, with affection and esteem, subscribes himself

YOURS EVER,

JAMES T. BRADY.

NEW YORK, *March* 26, 1860.

A Christmas Dream.

CHAPTER I

"NOT one cent."

"But please, sir, we haven't any bread at home."

"Not one cent, I say—begone!"

Yet it was Christmas Eve, and this sullen denial proceeded from one well provided with

7

the world's goods, toward a ragged and barefooted
girl, who, as she tramped over the cold pavement,
held out to the stony-hearted man a thin and tremu-
lous hand.

Yes! It was Christmas Eve, the anniversary of that
holy hour when we are taught that He was born,
who, turning aside from the great and the wealthy,
sought the abodes of the humble, and achieved his
most divine labors for man in relieving the loathsome
and degraded.

It was Christmas Eve, and the heart of a girl which
could have been made happy by the meanest coin
that ever oppresses the rags of a beggar, was by a
cold denial of the pitiful boon, sent cheerless out upon
the wide sea of selfishness, where if it should break
in agony, the event would no more attract the notice
of the multitude amidst which it happened, than the
bursting of a bubble would disturb the ocean.

It was Christmas Eve, and the streets were crowded
with happy people, who thronged about the various shops
to provide a jolly dinner for the morrow, or to purchase
presents for young folks who were destined to dream all

8

night of treasures, more valuable and vast than those which were displayed at the magic mention of "Open Sesame." Where the toys glittered in profusion, the boys were gathered at the door, wondering at the prices of what they were never to obtain, and gratifying their spirits by wishes that were never to be realized. In the windows of confectioners' shops, were exhibited the luscious and captivating preparations which were very likely soon to occasion busy employment for the family physician. Past all these the wretched girl wandered disconsolately, wearying herself still with the inquiry why others should be so blessed with all the means of pleasure, while she, in the prime of her life, knew little but sorrow and want. She had not yet become acquainted with Adam Smith's Wealth of Nations, nor investigated a report by the Secretary of the Treasury.

I had no time to pursue the person or fortunes of the girl. She disappeared suddenly in the tide of human beings that swept on in sullen monotony, even like the river which in its way to the ocean pauses not, whether the flower, the ripe fruit, the decayed tree, or the being full of life, fall on its rapid waters. My attention was arrested by the haggard features of a miserable *chiffonnier*, who, with a sack over his shoulder, and a hook in his hand, was journeying homeward after a day's vile labor in searching the kennels of the metropolis. A fur cap drawn far down to his eyes, left exposed a sharp brow, under which were hidden cavernous eyes that seemed to shrink from the foul work to which they were subjected. One would have thought while gazing on his

sunken cheeks, stern mouth, and projecting chin, that no smile had even, for one instant, lighted his sombre countenance. And yet who knows that he had not a hopeful and a happy youth in the "pleasant land of France," or the romantic home of the Switzer? It was hard to believe that the morose and melancholy wretch had ever been a child, and nestled in the arms of a devoted mother, while her fond eye shone upon his sweet slumber, like the evening star upon the dusky earth. But so it had been, no doubt, and possibly there were many who came at his birth to congratulate proud parents; hopes for a family's honor had perhaps grown strong as he progressed toward boyhood; he had haply been confided by a dying mother to the care of a merciful heaven, and sent out upon the world to seek his fortune, with the cheering encouragement of interested friends. To think that the child, which, fresh from Heaven, would have received the blessing of the Redeemer, if it had lived in the period of his benevolent mission, should thus be converted into a begrimed and wrinkled wretch, obtaining the means of existence from the very refuse of poverty!

"The world has more justice than we believe," remarked at this moment a gentleman passing me, to the friend at his side; and I knew from the speaker's look

and manner that the way of his life had been one of ease
and success, and that he knew no more of the fierce pas-
sions and dreadful wrongs that often convulse men's
frames, than the little rivulet, making its way century
after century through the solemn stillness of a primeval
forest, knows of the tempests that sweep the ocean in the
wildest nights.

A carriage passed me—the high-mettled horses at-
tached to which were controlled in their graceful and
spirited movements by a pompous coachman, who held

the reins delicately on the fingers of his white gloves,
while behind, a footman in lace and frippery looked over

the top of the vehicle as if in constant expectation that an acquaintance would come flying over the heads of the horses. Inside was the same churl who had refused the girl one copper, and it was plain that he had forgotten forever, except, perhaps, as the theme of an inflated discourse about "increasing pauperism," what I could not but remember as a striking illustration of those disparities which, while they must ever exist in life, can never fail to excite the regrets of all who wish that there could be less of suffering on earth, and more of real pleasure.

A terrible shriek arose from the pavement, and I saw the wheel of the churl's carriage pass over the leg of an unfortunate girl. The carriage stopped for a moment. The driver coolly inquired if any body were hurt; the crowd who had immediately assembled, told him to drive on, and I pushed toward the injured girl, just in time to see that it was she who had but a few minutes before elicited my sympathies, and that the coarse man who was holding her in his arms, and exclaiming in French, "My daughter," "My poor daughter," was the scavenger whose dismal face I had just encountered.

Even at the moment when the poor girl was borne into

a druggist's shop, and while the crowd stood gazing in, a
boy racing past exclaimed, as if the world depended on
his lungs:

"I wish you a merry Christmas, and a happy New
Year."

The crowd melted away from the apothecary's door,
the shuffle of the multitude went on in its old monotony,
the curses and shouts of omnibus drivers were heard
above the clatter of myriad wheels rattling over the
cobble stones, and I wended my way homeward, resolved
that I would on the morrow search for the unfortunate
girl, and see what might be done to relieve her. But the
sounds of music issuing from a fashionable restaurant
attracted my attention, and I went in.

We all know what a restaurant is in New York now;
with what elegance and costliness, if not taste, most
spacious "*salons à manger*" have been arranged, where
mirrors and polished white columns ornamented with
gold, and gay curtains with glittering loops, and cush-
ioned seats, invite to Apician suppers, with which the
most fastidious palate must be gratified.

I hid myself in one of the boxes, and modestly ordered

14

A CHRISTMAS DREAM.

some ale and a cigar, resolved to let the music which had lured me from my homeward path, harmonize with the thoughts which arose out of the strange episode in my life which had occurred from the accident to the girl, and the circumstances which preceded it.

Well, it has ever been so, and it must be so until the end of time. Poets and orators have complained that suffering too often attends the lives of those who, deprived of the means to make woe endurable, linger through a painful existence to a wretched end. And this should stimulate the faith and the hope of the skeptic in his heaviest and most cheerless despondency. It cannot be that the Almighty will not, at some time, and in his own inscrutable manner, equalize the disparities at which in this life we revolt. His omniscience—which, seeing through all the disguises of a corrupt nature, beholds the lecher in the priest, and the virgin spirit in the unfortunate harlot; he who knows how favorably the conscience that has yielded to strong temptations compares with that which never felt the necessity of resisting one dishonest impulse; he who beholds the injustice by which trembling innocence suffers at the bar where bloated arrogance pre-

sides; he who has his quick ear ready to catch the dying
murmur of the poor outcast, reluctant even in the last
agony to let the world that has rejected him know how
he feels its tyranny; he, in short, who knows the truth
and the right, and can exhume them though centuries of
falsehood and wrong be piled above, has some great
temple ready, where, under his own infallible guidance
that which was unjust on earth shall be remedied, and
those who suffered injustice shall be redressed.

All this while the four musicians performed a sweet
German melody, full of home and its associations,
a touching strain which convinced me that music de-
rives its power from harmonizing with those unuttered
thoughts of our deepest nature for which mere language
is inadequate. Yes! And it is but just there should be
a heaven in which those silent and unrevealed aspirations
of the spirit which can never be satisfied here, and at
which the world scoff, may find the pleasure for which
they long.

The ale was heavy withal, and my eyes drooped under
its unpoetical influence, so I left the lights, the Germans,
and the music, and would have made my way homeward,

A CHRISTMAS DREAM.

had I not been arrested at the door-step by a withered old man, very like the poor scavenger, but a little more neatly attired, who had a sack over his shoulder, and seemed hurried for time. As he expressed a wish to have some conversation with me, we passed back to the seat I had just left, and amidst the music, the clatter, and the smoke, took seats, and commenced gazing at each other with silent but absorbing interest.

(3)   17

CHAPTER II.

MY *vis à vis* was decidedly a strange character. It was difficult to detect the exact expression of his countenance, for it varied continually. Laying upon the table the sack I have mentioned, and opening it, he proceeded, with a very grave air, to produce a number of volumes, and arrange them with studious care.

"You will be surprised, sir," he remarked, "when I tell you who I am."

"Nothing can astonish me much in these days of magnetic telegraphs."

"But this is probably," said he, "the first time that you have had actual conversation with one who does not belong to this world, and is merely an agent of an absent monarch, to collect for him the trophies which increase with each succeeding moment."

I began to think my companion a madman, and the conviction was strengthened when he proceeded to say—

A CHRISTMAS DREAM.

"Yes! That monarch is the Past; an unrelenting and unyielding tyrant, who never returns the lightest trifle that ever comes within his grasp."

"And you," I remarked, "appear to be his confidential, clerk, or travelling agent."

"It is my duty," said the mysterious stranger, "to collect, during the brief period assigned for my labor, such mementos of his power as this earth may afford and when I shall have laid them at his feet, I, too, will become one of his victims and his monuments, and be denied the privilege of ever visiting this earth again."

"And what is your name?" I inquired.

"Alas!" exclaimed the stranger, "I am the 'Passing Year,' and although visible to you at this moment, have usually neither a 'local habitation' nor a name amongst mankind. I perceive that you are on the border line of life—that boundary between manhood and old age, at which the affections and feelings linger, the mind still looking backward to the scenes in which it knew the sweetest delights, while the flesh, growing weaker at every step, journeys toward eternity. In these volumes I have the record of what man has achieved during the

19

time of my pilgrimage—of the wrongs and virtues that have disfigured or adorned his career. It is a strange history of hopes that are blighted, friendships estranged, promises violated, faith disregarded, right trodden in the dust, wrong elevated to the highest places, merit spurned by the foot of presumption, and Virtue checked, and insulted by Vice in her flagrant and infamous career. Ob-

serve the comparative size of these volumes. Here," holding up a book not larger than a child's primer, "is the record of virtuous resolutions kept. What huge quarto enrolls those that were violated! The bad preponderates over the good through all these volumes in the same proportion. Ah, sir! mine has been an unpleasant duty. I was ushered into office amidst the wild shouts of the multitude hailing my approach, as if I were to bless them all with a profusion of Heaven's choicest gifts. Alas! many who shouted deliriously at my advent, are now low in the dust, and have been compelled to look on powerless, while death laid his icy hand upon some of the most generous hearts that ever thrilled within mortal bosom.

"I could tell you of one who seemed born to show how much that was immortal and noble could dwell within the precincts of a human frame. From childhood's earliest prime, to the moment when, far from friends and kindred, he breathed out his spirit to Heaven, there was no time when he stood in the path of any fellow-creature, or when there existed one wretch to whom his departure could afford a thrill of fiendish satisfaction. His heart was open to generous influences, as his countenance to the benign expressions which, beaming from every feature, cheered his troops of friends. There was no impulse of his soul, no word on his lip, no pressure in his hand,

21

that had ever felt the influence of hypocrisy, and in the prime of his manhood you might read his nature as easily as that of a child. Having nothing to conceal, he wondered that men were surprised at the frankness which was part of his nature; and he could not understand why, in association with his fellows, there could be a feeling called reserve. There were many, very many places where, without his ever knowing of his importance, the appearance of this benevolent and kindly being was hailed as the sufferer hails the ruddy dawn; and when he was striving to cheer the heavy hours of those who seemed to need his sympathy, how many hearts were eager to yield him the same solace! Full of boyish innocence, he yet plumed himself upon the ripe experience and practical wisdom of the man, assuming for the while, to give himself the weight that age and trial demand, an appearance of austerity which could but for a moment abide upon him, and which only served to amuse, like a grotesque mask concealing the features of a smiling face. In all that was generous, unselfish, and warm-hearted, he was, to most of his fellows, the wonder as well as idol; and there lives not one being who ever sought the influence of his kindly spirit, and went away dissatisfied. Men wondered that he did not yearn for fame; and yet, detecting himself in such a desire, he would have banished the thought at once, as involving a wish to elevate himself above those whom he loved. He would rather have the thanks of a beggar than the throne of Cæsar. But he has gone down into the grave, even when his friends strained the eyelids of their hearts for his coming and delighted in the expec-

tation that they must soon behold one who never grasped the hand of his fellow from any but a brother's feeling.

A CHRISTMAS DREAM.

He has gone, from no more apparent necessity than dies the bird which, during the sunny season, poured out its melodious song from the leafy spray, and has since uttered its last note in the wild-wood. He has gone, and all who knew him regret his departure, and feel that it is a greater trial to remain here, now that he is no more, than even to venture on the unknown world in quest of him, and the hearty greeting he knew how to give. If you ever feel a doubt that the beautiful and good exist hereafter, think of such a character as I have here described, and ask yourself if there can be one reason why such a being, having existed, should ever utterly perish. But I weary you with these saddening thoughts. It is Christmas Eve. Come forth with me into the air, and I will reveal to you what no mortal eye hath seen before. I will show you, in your own history, how is connected by a mysterious influence the Christmas of the present with the Christmas of the past."

24

CHAPTER III.

THERE is an elm-tree in the Park, near Chatham street, which, in the "golden prime" of my boyhood, was the *rendezvous* at which, after school hours and during holidays, we so often assembled, thence to set out on many a cheerful adventure in quest of fun. The merry group which clustered there so often, comes to my memory with the same distinctness as if by some magic influence I were carried backward over the intervening period to those happy school-boy days once more. I well remember that glorious period, during which, unlike almost all my companions, I did not lose the enjoyment of present happiness in the strange ambition to be a man. All my wants were then provided for by those whom it has been my lot to see laid in the dust. Oh! how at the hour when school was "dismissed" we scampered off as wild caprice suggested, making the street resound with jocund shouts, and engaging in the various sports which youth so ingeniously devises. There was an ogre, too, in those days— the keeper of the park—a mild and worthy man in his ordinary mood, no doubt, but with a nose that blushed scarlet over the transgressions of his lips. We gave him the title of "Rum-nose," which, perhaps, was more just than elegant, and it was our great delight to annoy the poor fellow, leading him into useless chases up and down the steps of the City Hall, and through its entries, over its vestibule, and even into the court-rooms, where justice is said to be administered. Christmas Eve was a great time then, and was seen from afar. We commenced discussing its advent, and the delights it would bring, from the last holiday that preceded it; and even now, when in the maturity of life we find Christmas at hand, and feel no excitement of preparation, we wonder why we miss the feverish expectation with which it was once awaited, forgetting how few cares we had then to disturb the darling anticipation of the heart. How delightful then became the home from which we had so often stolen out at nights in defiance of parental authority, and to the imminent danger of our persons! There was such a "busy note of preparation" about the house, such mys-

A CHRISTMAS DREAM.

terious deposits of turkeys and quarters of mutton in the hall, such strange developments of baskets, only equalled by the banquets that come from the earth in pantomime, and such a profusion of fruit and confections actually left within our reach without even a prohibition to touch them. Who can even forget the smell of his Christmas home?

"There is the Christmas table of your youth," said my companion; and lo! I had become a boy again. The dinner table was surrounded by the family once more. There was not even one absent. He "by whose kind, paternal side" we grew toward manhood, occupied the head of the table, his hair slightly dashed with gray, his face radiant with a cheerful smile, and his proud glance directed around the abundant board to those on whom his hopes and pride now centred. And there was, too, my mother—she of whom the recollection, now that she has been some years "laid in her narrow place of rest," is like a mingled sense of pleasure and duty, each ever present, and each in turn growing stronger than its kindred feeling—she to whom, in my earliest sufferings, I breathed my secret complaints with the sublime con-

27

fidence that they were as safe as they could be in
Heaven—she whose ready ear caught up every syllable
in which I told of any wrong her son had suffered, or
honor he had attained, however evanescent—she, whose
large heart, peopled by her children, seemed yet capa-
cious enough to nurture all the afflicted of the human

A CHRISTMAS DREAM.

race—she, whose face now, in the greatest anguish of
manhood, comes like an angel from God to my spiritual
sense, and whispers, in language which the soul only can
hear, that there will be a season of relief and of happiness—she, the dearly beloved idol of my whole nature,
whose hand still seems to have smoothed my pillow
when I lie down for rest on earth, whose presence shall
be felt in each thrill of my latest breathings at the
solemn hour of death, and who I know will be the first
to meet me, if we be restored to each other by the
benign mercy of a benevolent God.

There, too, about that table, were all my brothers and
sisters. All were in perfect health, and all happy. Such
eating, drinking, laughing, singing, and after the dinner,
such dancing, tumbling, and playing at Blindman's Buff!
The scene went swimming before me, and in an instant
the whole of a past life was disclosed.

"The Christmas of manhood," said my companion.

The same table, with no diminished store of what may
yield the body pleasure, but, oh! how much narrowed
the happy circle which once gathered there at the happy
Christmas season! He was gone, the pillar and the prop

of all; gone in the maturity of life, but before the frosts
of age had been laid too deep on the generous impulses
that burned in his magnanimous nature. She, too, had
departed, at whose decease it seemed so unwise that any
should be permitted to remain, and in the absence of
whom the rose seemed to have lost its fragrance, and the
very stars their glory. A sister, too, whose graceful form
moved like a thing of light and pleasure through the
household, gladdening wherever it came—her chair also
was vacant. And now that I observe more closely, I
miss the face of him whose features seemed to flash from
them in combined light all of good and pleasant that
existed in all the family beside. Death, alas! had
"stepped in and thinned that little band," and the members of the circle, once so extended, now drew closer and
closer together, because of the breaches that had been
made in their ranks, to sustain each other, until, at the
command of him who gives and takes away, the last link
of the chain shall, I trust, be reunited with that from which
it was wrested when the first of our dear ones perished·

"My time is drawing near to its close," said the Passing Year, "and I have but one more scene to show you."

30

A CHRISTMAS DREAM.

There was the parlor of our home. The fire, that I had expected to see burning cheerfully when I returned, had a dim look, and, strange to say, four figures sat around it holding correspondence with each other, with looks that indicated conversation, but were unattended with any sounds. How can I describe the pleasure that pervaded each pulse of my frame, when I recognized the dear departed members of our family enjoying, as they were wont to do in life, the comforts of that home which their presence had so often made happy! How ecstatic would my joy have been could I have embraced them all; but the hand of my attendant was laid upon me, and I could but gaze upon my heavenly visitors, rapt in wonder and delight.

"They have been waiting for you to come home," said he; "and will not quit the house until you are secure in slumber. Look!"

I gazed with astonishment while my dear lost ones ascended to the rooms where our family repose, and saw each of them stoop over those who were sleeping, to kiss the slumberer's cheek. Then all stood around the bed and elevated their eyes with their prayers to our Maker.

31

A CHRISTMAS DREAM.

Then they returned to the fire, and seated themselves once more, and there came back to my delighted spirit such a sensitive recollection of all they had done for me, and of what I had omitted that might have made their lives more happy, that I could have fallen on my knees before them and besought the forgiveness of each. But I was restrained by my companion; and it was not until I had laid myself down to rest for the night that the beloved faces visited my couch also, and lingered over my pillow with looks of undying love. Then I heard the prayers for my prosperity, mingled with sounds of sweetest melody, which seemed to combine expression of all the memories that followed my steps from childhood to the present hour.

The benign faces of the dear ones disappeared, but my old companion stood beside my bed and, laying his hand upon mine, said, in a voice whose every tone still lingers in my memory:

"You have seen to-night the appeal of suffering spurned by the heartlessness of bloated avarice. You have seen what would be the rank injustice of a world controlled by blind chance, where, if the afflicted child were crushed beneath the wheel of the miser, there could be no redress for the one, nor punishment for the other.

"You have been assured by visions that those whom you loved above all others on earth, still follow, and are with you, and watch over you when slumber is sweetest. These have not been the visions of a waking sense, but mysterious revelations from your heart, teaching the sublime lesson that the influence which any beloved object once gained over your nature will survive the decease of the object itself; and if you do but cherish it a little, will be as a fragrance shed upon your soul to make it pure forever. Wake on the morrow, and conduct your life as if it had been disclosed to you that they whose good opinion you so respected while they lived, are still near to the dear ones whom they nurtured, and for whose prosperity they were ready even to lay down life. The ancients had their household gods—the work of mortal hands, and only sanctioned by the sincerity of superstition—while you, through the blessing of Heaven, enjoy the omnipresent care of the great Creator, and have, as gods of the household, the memories of departed loved ones, to be reunited with whom should be the aim and end of your whole existence. Ponder this well, and feel the solemn truth which it was my mission to disclose, that in the midst of happiest life, and when the thoughts of death are furthest from your heart, there may be, close beside you, eager with care lest you should by some false step be lost from the path that may lead you to their arms, those for whose presence in another world you should pray most fervently to your Maker."

I know not how my mysterious visitor departed, nor where. But he made my Christmas more cheerful than it would have been but for his teachings. I communicate the lesson he imparted to me, with the hope that even with as much pleasure as descends upon one ray of sunshine into the prisoner's cell, it may fall on the heart of those who have recently suffered a domestic affliction. There must be many who at this festive season will be compelled to steal away from the pleasures of general hospitality, and who will spend the hours, that were in happier times devoted to heartfelt pleasure, in the society of the dead and not of the living. To these even my words may be like the rain-drops on the parched earth, and I would say to them that it may, perhaps, occasion

34

anguish to those they love and have lost, to see them indulging sorrow that is useless, although grateful, and that they should rather spend in mild pleasure the hours of that holiest season when He came to bless the earth, through whom we are taught that the dead and the living may meet and be happy again.

— — —

Eighteen hundred and sixty! And lo! the Christmas time again returns. Fifteen eventful years have passed away since I cast thee—frail offering—upon the waters of literature, little dreaming that thou would'st come back to me, even "after many days." But it is the season when many a wanderer revisits home, and why should'st not thou cease to be a truant? Welcome, slender "birth of my thought"—memorial of the by-gone days with which so many cheerful and saddening associations are now connected. Industry and art have sent thee to me in guise more attractive far than that in which thou first went forth, and I behold the beauty of thy dress with pleasure. Let me fold this new garment of affectionate

35

A CHRISTMAS DREAM.

words about thee, and prepare thee once more for a journey into the wide, wide world.

It has been said that after thirty, we make no new friends. Few have failed to verify, in their experience, the general truth of the aphorism. And it may be an illustration of this truth, that even in journeying toward the fortieth year of existence, we advance often with eyes cast backward, lingering with affectionate constancy amidst the acquaintances and incidents of our prime. A lock of hair, a ring, a word penned by some beloved hand —the merest trifle, casually encountered, may recall the hour when it first came to our touch. We fondle in memory over the memorial sometimes with tearful hearts. And why may not this little book call up some tribute from my sensibilities, when I behold in it the record of that era when not one touch of frost had assailed my brow, nor experience yet instructed me to distrust the whispers of Hope or the promises of Ambition?

Fifteen eventful years! terminating at the period when the onward march of life is inevitably and rapidly toward indifference, infirmity, and death! The hours now flit away as instants, the seasons chase each other with rapid

A CHRISTMAS DREAM.

feet, and the years grow shorter and shorter. We who feel these truths—let us look back over the interval I have mentioned. The children, in whose sweet prattle we once delighted, have long since forgotten that imperfect speech which surpasses perfect elocution, and have grown to glib maturity. Ella no longer sits on our lap and hears our stories of the nursery, or the Fairy realms. She was then

> "Pure as the hues within the flower,
> To summer and the sun unknown."

Even so pure is the darling now, but the world has touched her nature, and the resistless current of fashion drawn her within its flow. She is the beloved of some gallant gentleman, no doubt, who will monopolize all the sweet favors which her young lips were wont to lavish on many cherishing admirers. Ben, who was so formidable on his cane, which he bestrode as if it were a Bucephalus, to charge, like *Cœur de Lion*, castles made of chairs, in which imaginary ogres imprisoned lovely virgins—Ben swells the ranks of " Young America," knows the flavor of every vintage—the reputation of every *cuisine*; is eloquent upon *Chateau Margaux* and " Figaros ;" discourses politics, science, and art ; is didactic at times about " human nature;" and when the dance goes on, performs in a minute more revolutions than were ever thought of on the continent. Our contemporaries—they who a few years since showed glossy locks of all hues but silver—how grizzly and dry they appear these cool mornings. We begin to doubt whether it is safe to associate with the old fellows. But are they all here to-day? Alas! where is he with whom so often in athletic exercise I sought the rest and recreation most welcome after hours of toil, and in whose company so many of the smaller hours were passed, mingling revelry, I fear, with strange and versatile discourse? Where he with whom I first sought the shores of the Old World, grateful that we might tread together the " pleasant land of France," the vine-clad fields of Italy, the green sward of the British Islands, in hours that seem covered all over with the garlands of memory? Where he who, full of even audacious energy, was my associate or my opponent in those struggles from which fame was anticipated, if not won, and whose active brain and form challenged alike the admiration of foe or friend? The premature grave and the unrelenting sea must give the sad responses to my call. Alas! how I shudder when

3*

A CHRISTMAS DREAM.

the past discloses to my mind's eye those, too, who, failing to achieve any part of the triumphs for which they had every endowment, went down so ignobly in the " battle of life," leaving Charity to be the kindest and best guardian of their memory. Alas ! too—how many have departed full of the honors which it might seem just that they should enjoy forever, even in mortal existence ; they whose old age was not less beautiful than their youth, and " every wrinkle on whose brows was but a notch in the calendar of a well-spent life."

Yet who shall repine at these, the common results of our sublunary drama—these many parts and dooms ex-hibited in the great theatre of humanity ? Why repeat so tediously the lamentations which, in every tongue, and far more eloquent phrase than mine, have been uttered ever since man's voice was heard on earth ? Did I not say that the Christmas time returns ? Here is the jocund season ; the evergreens are gathered to deck the halls of hospitable homes ; the members of families, separated for months or years, are once more to assemble around the familiar hearth-stones ; the banquet and the music are being prepared ; the flowers are already wreathed ; the

memories awakened; the ears and hearts attuned to
symphonies; and while the lights gleam, and the strains
of melody mingle in the brilliant atmosphere with de-
licious perfume, the laugh of age shall unite with that of
childhood, the feast shall be ample, the jest swift, the
dance nimbler than ever, and the hours go round with
only lustre on their wings. Go to! Let us leave off this
useless sorrowing. What though the past exhibits a path
tracked with the tombs of beloved ones whose hearts,
that once throbbed in unison with ours, have long since
mouldered? What though the circle of friends from
which so much of illumination radiated upon our souls,
grows narrower, and we doubt whether, when the next
of its links is broken, we shall share or occasion the sorrow of survivors? Yet should we be of good cheer, and
snatch from passing Time whatever innocent grace or
pleasure he places within our grasp. We are the recruits
of the vast army which has moved for ages onward to a
common fate—units of that

" Innumerable caravan
Which moves to that mysterious realm,
Where each must take his chamber
Within the silent halls of Death."

A CHRISTMAS DREAM.

Our brothers in the pilgrimage will fall at our side, but however thickly the arrows of death may shower, we can, while our powers continue, do naught but move on until we reach the awful instant when we are to exchange the feeble pulses of transitory existence for the ceaseless throbbings of eternal life. There, even there, at that mysterious frontier, if we have been faithful and fearless in the march, we may lie down obedient to destiny, with the exalted hope that after all the objects of this world shall have become lost forever to our mortal sight, there may be unfolded to our new and spiritual vision another realm of unimaginable glory, where we and all whom we loved on earth may realize the promise which the Great Ruler of the universe has made unto the just.

CHRISTMAS, 1860.

www.ingramcontent.com/pod-product-compliance
Lightning Source LLC
Chambersburg PA
CBHW020817030726
47496CB00009B/2931